The Green Gummy Man

by Liza Charlesworth
illustrated by Claudio Cerri

ISBN: 979-8-225-02080-4

Publisher: Tara Welty
Creative Director: Tannaz Fassihi; Designer: Cynthia Ng

1 2 3 4 5 6 7 8 9 10 68 34 33 32 31 30 29 28 27 26 25

Made in Jiaxing City, China. First printing, August 2025.

SCHOLASTIC

This spooky tale begins with an old woman. The woman had a home deep in the woods. To pass the time, she made yummy treats. She made mints, lollipops, and candy canes. Best of all, she made a big gummy man. The gummy man was green and squishy.

He had a coat and pants and a fine top hat. The green gummy man seemed quite polite. As he cooled on a plate, he tipped his hat at the woman and said, “It is nice to meet you.” “It is nice to meet you as well,” she replied. “You are way too sweet to ever be eaten.” Then she turned off the light and went to bed.

But the gummy man was not what he seemed.
As soon as the old woman started to snore,
he grabbed a candy cane and ran out the door.
The sky was black and the moon was full.
“Hee, hee! I am free!” he giggled with glee.
“It is time for me to explore the world!”

The gummy man walked in the dark woods.
He saw trees and plants and creepy bugs.
Then he saw two furry paws with claws.
Yikes! They belonged to a bobcat on the prowl.
"Growl!" said the bobcat. "I think I just
found the perfect late-night snack."

“I think NOT,” replied the gummy man.
Then, off he dashed, singing this little tune:
“Silly bobcat, run as fast as you can.
But you cannot chomp the gummy man!”
Did the bobcat chase the man? Yes!
Did the bobcat catch the man? No!

After a while, the bobcat gave up and
the gummy man returned to his walk.
Looking up, he spotted two brown wings.
Oh my! They belonged to a screech owl.
"Hoot!" said the screech owl. "I just spotted
my next meal, and it looks quite yummy."

"No meal for you!" yelled the gummy man.
Then, off he dashed, singing this little tune:
"Silly screech owl, flap as fast as you can.
But you cannot gobble the gummy man!"
Did the screech owl chase the man? Yes!
Did the screech owl catch the man? No!

After a while, the screech owl gave up and the gummy man returned to his walk. By and by, he came to a wide stream. That's when he spotted two yellow eyes. Yikes! They belonged to a furry red fox. A fox beside a stream was a big problem!

“Greetings, gummy man,” said the red fox.
“Do not be afraid. I don’t like to eat sweets.
But I do like to help. Hop on my back and
I will take you safely across the stream.”
Was the fox telling the truth or being sly?

Hmmm? The green gummy man did not know.
But he REALLY needed to cross the stream.
So, he replied, "OK!" and hoped for the best.
Then he jumped on the fox's furry back.
Paddle, paddle! The fox swam and swam.

After a while, the stream got quite deep
and the fox said, “It is not fun to get wet.
You will be much safer on top of my head.”
Was the fox telling the truth or being sly?
Hmmm? The green gummy man did not know.
But he REALLY needed to stay dry,
so he took the red fox’s advice.

One, two, three—time to leap!
It was mid-leap when the gummy man found out the truth. The red fox's mouth was wide open and he was drooling A LOT! That sly fox had lied. He DID like sweets. He DID plan to eat the green gummy man.

"I am not food!" blurted the gummy man.
"I need a way to save myself—and quick!"
So, he whacked the fox with his candy cane.
Then when his enemy yelped in pain,
the gummy man took a HUGE leap. . .
and lucky him. He landed on a log!

Yippee! The green gummy man was safe.
As the log floated off, he sang this little tune:
“Silly red fox, play all the tricks you can.
But you cannot munch the gummy man!”
After a while, the log got stuck in a patch
of thick weeds beside a stone path.
Where did that stone path lead?

Right back to the home of the old woman who'd made him! What did he do next? One, two, three—leap! He got on his plate before that old woman even woke up. Did the green gummy man plan to tell her about his spooky walk in the woods? Nope! He was VERY good at keeping secrets.